RENDEZVOUS

by

Nowick Gray

World Castle Publishing, LLC

WCP

World Castle Publishing, LLC
Pensacola, Florida

Copyright © Nowick Gray 2013
ISBN: 9781939865687
First Edition World Castle Publishing, LLC September 1, 2013
http://www.worldcastlepublishing.com

Licensing Notes

Editor: Maxine Bringenberg

Cover based on original artwork by Rowena Eloise, depicting Jumbo Pass, the real-life setting for Rendezvous. As this pristine wilderness area faces the threat of massive development, please consider supporting the Jumbo Wild campaign: http://www.keepitwild.ca/about-jumbo

Chapter One

The cabin appears in the distance, nestled beside a half-frozen pond. It's a scene from an old-fashioned Christmas card—except the cabin's chimney pipe shows no smoke. "Looks like we're the first ones here," I say to Matt. I check my watch again.

My companion bends forward with the weight of his pack. He rests his hands on his knees, catching his breath. "Yeah—what time is it?"

"Twenty past three."

"Well, we're behind schedule from losing our trail. They could have had the same trouble on the other side."

"Yeah; or maybe they got a late start."

Matt turns his eyes from me toward the

cabin. Sweat generated from our last steep climb up the scree slope drips from his limp, wet mustache.

I start to shiver. It's the end of June, but at six thousand feet, a sweating body cools quickly. "Maybe they're already in the cabin and there's no wood; or they just got there and haven't lit a fire yet."

We trudge on through wet, foot-deep snow to the cabin. A couple of wooden steps at the entrance are falling apart; otherwise, the rustic structure appears stoutly built, with walls of rough planks supported by a stone foundation.

I push open the creaking door; wind whips into the single room. The cabin is well equipped, for all its remoteness. A neat pile of split firewood sits stacked beside a little stove. I notice plenty of blankets, sleeping bags, and spare shoes on a drying rack overhead, and four built-in bunks complete with foam mattresses. In the kitchen cupboards we find matches, toilet paper, tea, cocoa, soup packets, and a bag of rice, along with a portable camp stove and fuel, cookware, and dishes.

Matt unlaces his wet boots and suggests we start a fire to dry our clothes and heat water for tea. Anxious for the arrival of the other party, I tell him to go ahead; I'll scout around to see if I can see or hear a sign of their approach. He tries to reassure me that they're probably just running late. I leave him to the stove and take off, with map in hand, for the end of the ridge, calling out and peering down into the dim vastness of the Tumbler Creek drainage.

There is no response to my shouts in the empty wind. Far down the mountainside, the creek streams out from its source ice fields and winds away beyond my sight. Somewhere in the labyrinth of trees and ridges, a trail runs along the slope, veering up for a final ascent to the pass. My wife Faron and three-year-old daughter Suze are now over half an hour late for our long-planned rendezvous at Mirror Pass. There I stand, hearing the echo of my shouts and gazing at the wilderness, its beauty so desolate and incomplete.

Chapter Two

Morning light drew our eyelids slowly open. I pulled Faron closer while we still had the chance.

"Nine weeks," she said in a forlorn whisper. "Nine weeks too long."

As soon as our lips touched, Suze awoke from her bed beside us, right on cue. No turning the clock back now.

Never had I been away from Faron for longer than a week in our four years together. Now we would have to last four or five weeks at a stretch, until I could arrange a quick trip back home for a couple of days between shifts. The tree planting camp would be a full day's drive away, in the next valley.

But when John Harris had called me with a

job offer, I told him sure thing. Who wouldn't, with a half-finished house and a three-year-old to raise? The house was a full forty feet long, but so far, only fourteen feet wide, like an overgrown trailer, or a glorified railway shed. The exposed hallway served as a temporary outer wall, showing not one but a row of doors. Each door led to a promised interior room, but for now, each gave access to the same undivided living area.

We got up and dressed; then Faron fried pancakes while I finished packing. Over breakfast and a road map, we calculated how many round-trips our budget could bear, feeding the gas-guzzling Ford. Expecting to pull in a hundred and fifty dollars a day, I wasn't concerned over the odd trip home.

Faron was more prudent: "Remember all the other things we need that money for, Will; those planting days have to cover us for the whole year."

"Yeah, I know, but—"

"Hey, I know how we could do it!"

Uh-oh, I thought with a flinch. *She's got that adventurous gleam in her eye.*

"You're going to be up near Inverness in a

couple of weeks, directly across the mountains from here."

"Yeah, that's kind of neat."

"More than neat, Will. Look on the map. Mirror Pass, right up there. If there's a trail on the east side, you could hike over the pass on a day off and meet me on the Tumbler Creek side."

"That's true. You could drive up to the trail—if the road's open—and pick me up. It would take me a whole day to get home, though. If I happened to score two days off, I'd have to head right back over the next morning, and then work another shift with no rest. We wouldn't have much time together; just the overnight."

Faron leaned onto a muscular forearm, her jaw set. This meant one thing…there had to be a way; and if not, she'd push one through. "Look, it's so close, on the map."

I had no solution to offer, other than driving the long way around.

Her eyes lit up. "Hey, I've got it. You hike up your side, and I'll come up the trail from the west, and we'll meet at the pass. There's a cabin there, where we can stay the night. We'll have more time together that way."

I pictured our bed, not in the cabin but out under the millions of stars wheeling around amid the frosted peaks. "Hmmm. I wonder. Maybe it's not such a crazy scheme after all."

Suze had stopped stuffing pancake in her mouth long enough to attempt speech...or at least a strangled whimper, muted yet effective.

It brought me back to earth. I spoke for the little tyke before she choked. "But Faron, what do we do about Suze?"

"Oh, I'm sure she'd love to come."

"I'm sure she would." Suze vigorously nodded her head, her bulging cheeks stained with huckleberry syrup. "But how's she going to get there? It's what—a three-hour hike for an adult, in shape?"

"She could walk up part of the way."

"And have you carry her the rest? Wouldn't it be easier to find someone she could stay with?"

"Oh, she'd rather come—wouldn't you, Suze?"

When Suze hesitated, Faron added, "We'll bring lots of food along; and your bluey quilt."

"Yessee, yessee, I wanna come."

And so our plan was hatched.

***

My good-bye was the easier of the two. I had the excitement of a trip and new experiences to look forward to. Faron would be left at home with Suze and the big garden to look after; and on top of it, she'd also taken on the job of babysitting two other kids.

Backpacking around Europe at seventeen, running a printing press at nineteen, roaming the mountains for a week in her twentieth year, and having our child at twenty-one: these all came naturally to her. With Faron it was a matter of style, pace. On a morning off from more widespread obligations, she could conjure a whirlwind in the kitchen yielding a batch of bread, a couple of dozen quarts of canned fruit, and several pies—with a cord of firewood split and stacked, between infrequent peeks in the oven. One or two burned pies...the cost of accomplishment.

As we held each other one last time by the brown truck door, Faron cried. I smoothed the wet strands of hair to the sides of her cheeks, encircled her arching back to pull her closer, and took her mouth to mine. Then I got into the truck, tried to smile for her, and rumbled down the driveway.

Chapter Three

From my first day of work I began to dream of the future rendezvous. Packing fifty-pound tree bags up and down the razed slopes and gnarly ravines, through logging slash and rockslides, fighting duff and sod and rock and flies, my body took a beating and my mind sought solace elsewhere. I filled the mindless dimension of the work with visions of Faron: her sparkling almond eyes, her sweet lips, her body made fit by the chores of homesteading.

But the quality of my work suffered. Daydreams of the distant peaks turned to nightmares under my nose as I had to spend two days replanting whole sections of ground: digging up each of hundreds of seedlings and packing them back in the earth, firmer, straighter, deeper.

Somehow two weeks passed, and that hellish first contract was finished. No one had made much money. A dozen planters had quit or been lamed. After days of blistering heat, it snowed the day we broke camp. I worried about my truck with no chains getting down the winding dirt roads. Dispirited by these realities, I began to doubt the feasibility of a fanciful mountaintop honeymoon.

A ragtag caravan of assorted vehicles carrying forty surviving planters and all our camp gear—kitchen and shower trailers, collapsible tent-shacks for drying clothes and for dining, all our tree bags, tapered shovels, spiked boots, rainwear—proceeded up the valley to set up again for the more promising five-week Grand Creek contract.

I took the occasion of a supper stop in Inverness to phone Faron. Beyond the essential I-miss-you's and I-love-you's, she had news to report. She'd taken an exploratory trip up the western route to the pass, accompanied by Karianne, a woman whose husband, David, was part of my crew. The idea was to make the hike a double date. They took Karianne's small horse along in the back of our old Dodge half-ton truck as a means of carrying Suze and Karianne's two kids up the trail.

The Tumbler Creek road was in such bad shape, Faron told me, that they had to stop and move rocks in several places along the way, from slides that half-covered the road. On the creek side were steep drop-offs.

"I was terrified," Faron told me.

I asked her why they didn't turn around and go back home.

"Turn around! Are you kidding? That would have been worse, to try to back up far enough to find a wide spot for turning around. You know how it is for me to try to drive in reverse."

"Yeah, you're right." She could only reach the pedals in a normal driving position with the help of two pillows propped behind her back. "So what did you do?"

"Well, Karianne got out, with all the kids of course, and tried to guide me through. She seemed to think I had lots of room. But I couldn't see anything—except air on one side, and rock on the other. My hands were shaking so hard I could barely hang onto the steering wheel."

It didn't work out very well, for all that. There were too many logs that the horse couldn't get over; and even after continuing on foot, they were turned back by old, unmelted snow on the upper reaches of the trail.

So Faron's sturdy, five-foot-two frame would have to be fit for the task of carrying Suze at least part of the way up. She still sounded determined to make a go of it. I promised to keep in touch as I found out more about the road and trail at my end.

***

The caravan turned west from Inverness into the mountains. Halfway along this last road we passed the plush Columbiana Alpine Resort, and the pavement turned to dirt and gravel. This would be the closest outpost of civilization—if civilization is tennis courts, hot tubs, a telephone, and a bar. The new campsite, located an hour's drive along Grizzly Creek, lay at the point where Grand Creek roared in.

At the confluence of the two major creeks, a flat clearing served as a base camp for a hunting guide, who had given advance permission for us to stay there. Of course, the very evening of our arrival, the guide showed up with his horses and clients; and so our brightly colored tents, which had just sprouted in his corral like so many exotic mushrooms, had to be moved to the woods. The hunters had come for grizzly. Early the next morning they saddled up, with their rifles ready in their leather cases, and rode off in the direction of Mirror Pass.

Beyond camp, the dirt road narrowed and stretched up the Grand Creek valley for twelve more kilometers. The planting blocks rose up the east slopes from the road. Mirror Pass beckoned invisibly, tantalizingly from around the last mountain in sight.

As we traveled each day in the crew trucks that took us to work, I began to plan for the day I would drive my own truck to the end of the road, where the trail to the pass began. When I broached the idea to Harris, my towering, intimidating boss, he told me that the road was reportedly washed out somewhere past the last planting blocks. There was a possibility, he said, that it had been patched since.

"But if not," I was happy to hear him say, "you could take one of the boony bikes. I'll check out the situation one day when I'm up that way." He enjoyed bouncing around on the balloon-tired, all-terrain, motorized "trikes," and I was glad to have the big man's support for my little adventure.

Two weeks went by. On the better ground there, I became preoccupied with trees, time, and money. Never mind the dazzling vistas of glaciated peaks from the higher slopes. I could look at them during lunch. On and on I pushed myself, faster, faster...stride, stride, tree; stride, stride, tree...my shovel and I a hybrid machine. Up and down the mountainsides, all day long in a race against time, I pounded in the seedlings, up to a thousand a day. At twenty cents a crack, I couldn't afford to think about Faron.

Back in camp at the end of a day, when my stomach was filled and conversation became sparse and stale, my thoughts would return to her. As time wore on, past the third week, into the fourth and fifth, I ached with a visceral emptiness that all the good camp food couldn't begin to fill. I'd plod over to my plywood box (the Ford's homemade camper/canopy), brush my teeth in the fading light, and crawl into my bed of foam pads and sleeping bags, diverting my mind until dark with a good mystery or Stephen King novel. It was the dimly formed vision of Faron's face, though, and the disembodied love behind her ever-cheerful smile, that would haunt me into sleep.

Faron and I still had a plan, of sorts. We just had to wait until the end of the contract, because until then Harris was unwilling to give the crew more than one day off at a time. That magical date was impossible to pin down, meanwhile, because of inconsistent daily planting totals and a mysteriously indeterminate number of remaining seedlings.

Related to the problem of timing was the problem of access. The road was indeed washed out beyond repair, Harris had found, not far past the last cut-blocks. The boony bike "might" make it, he told me, if the right place to cross were found. There were other complications, however.

Pressure was mounting on Harris to finish this contract and move to the next one. That meant the off-days coming up would be needed to break and move the camp. I could probably wrangle out of that obligation, but the boony bikes would have to go with the camp. That left me with my truck. There were numerous minor washouts on the way, which we crossed daily in the crew trucks only with a good deal of scraping, bouncing, churning, and plain dumb luck. These freshets were increasing in volume every day in the sweltering June sun.

I needed a backup plan. So after work one evening, with less than a week to go in the contract, I looked into mountain bike rentals from the Columbiana resort.

***

Summer was off-season at what was primarily a ski resort. I wandered through the deserted buildings until I found someone who could tell me about their rental bikes. They were available only on Sundays and Tuesdays, cost twenty-five dollars a day, and had no panniers. I took this information to the bar terrace and sat for half an hour over a watery draft beer, scribbling out a bewildering matrix of dates, distances, risks and benefits, pros and cons. Maybe this harebrained scheme, I was starting to think, just wasn't in the cards.

Getting nowhere, I phoned Faron. Her plans were complicated by trying to arrange days off from babysitting, and to find someone to come along on the hike. The basic idea was to have help carrying Suze. The so-called "double-date" idea had fallen through; David had decided he'd had enough of Harris's whip cracking, and had left in the morning to drive home. Faron's best bet at that point was a friend and neighbor, Ron; but he hadn't made a final commitment as yet. I told Faron that a fellow planter named Matt had expressed interest in accompanying me.

"Oh?" she said. "What's he like?"

"Why do you want to know?"

"Just curious. He will be sharing the cabin with us, after all."

"Okay—he's tall, dark, and handsome, and a helluva planter. He flails away at the slash and duff like some six-foot-five bear. Let's see, what else? He has black hair and a beard. He's a theology student. And he just broke up with his girlfriend Janet, who's—"

"Woman friend, you mean. Or just 'friend.'"

"Whatever. She is pretty attractive, herself. She's been planting, and tenting, with Matt all season. But now it looks like that's finished. Matt says he's ready for a break, something more challenging than the usual days off hanging around camp or town."

Faron said, "It won't be quite the same as just us, up there together."

"It wouldn't be just us, anyway, with Suze there, and whoever you get to come with you."

"That's true."

"Anyway, it still makes sense for both of us to go with someone."

"I know. Ron was telling me that Mirror Pass is called the grizzly capital of the world."

"Oh, great. Well, I hope he decides to come along. Bears or no bears, anything could happen."

"We'll be all right."

Was that just her characteristic confidence at work, I wondered, or some greater understanding that was not yet clear to me?

"I'll take your word for it, sweetie."

By the end of the call, Faron's voice was shaky with emotion. "Will you call me again as soon as you find out more about your days off?"

"For sure. I can't wait!" I realized as I said this how true it was for me, and I also realized the truth about Faron's approach to difficulty:

you just had to want something like this badly enough to make it happen, one way or another.

There was a long, palpable silence. Then Faron said, "I guess we should hang up. We're spending all the money you're making."

"Yeah, isn't it terrible? But it's worth it. Bye—I love you, Faron."

"I love you, too, Will."

Chapter Four

The hope of finishing the contract on that last full day of work, a Saturday, spurred everyone on. I started highballing, and in the process lost the line of planted trees I was supposed to be following. *The hell with it*, I said to myself—and ended up planting a single line of trees on a beeline into nowhere. When finished with the run of four hundred, I tried to get my bearings, bushwhacking over ridges while calling out for signs of humanity (watching out, meanwhile, for a rumored rogue moose, a mother separated from her calf) until I finally stumbled into a tree cache. Alex, my gray-bearded supervisor, calmly looked up from his cup of coffee and said in his best Texas drawl, "Doctor Livingstone, I presume?"

Despite the crew's collective best efforts, a few dozen boxes of trees remained in the caches at the end of the day. That was just as well, because now there was a large unplanted hole to fill between my errant line and the main section of planted trees.

Sunday a partial crew of volunteers would finish up. I chose not to work, resting and preparing for the hike. Monday the camp would come down and be moved; and Tuesday, Harris announced, would be a full day off before the next contract.

I hopped in the crew truck with the radiophone and drove down the road to the one point where radio waves could find a hole in the wall of mountains. When I reached Faron, our voices and breathy silences pulsed wondrously in the crackling airwaves. Our timing was perfect: she'd already arranged to be free on Monday and Tuesday, and today she was preparing for the trip.

I spent the rest of the day packing and helping out with the initial stages of breaking camp. I also finalized plans with Matt, an experienced mountaineer whose judgment I trusted. He thought, and I was willing to agree, that the big truck had enough clearance and guts to rumble over the washouts. We would try to take the truck as far as the major washout, eight kilometers up the road. From there we could easily walk the last four kilometers to the trail. As for the return trip, we would aim for arriving back at the truck by four-thirty on Tuesday. Harris didn't have a definite location for the new camp yet, so we'd have to phone the forest company office from Columbiana before they closed, in order to know where to go that night. Then it would be touch and go to make it to Inverness, because my truck only had a quarter-tank of gas, and Harris couldn't spare any from his marginal supplies.

***

Monday morning the washouts were definitely deeper. We barreled through on the first one, wide spray and all. But just out of the second one the Ford's engine stalled. It seemed a bad sign. I wondered once more if this romantic adventure just wasn't meant to be, if perhaps all these minor obstacles had been placed in our path by a higher authority. Couldn't I take a hint? But then I thought of Faron, pushing on with her end of the journey from the west, and I was determined to find a way through to join her as we'd planned.

The truck wouldn't start again. Matt and I tried gas pedal, air cleaner, choke, spark plugs, and just waiting. I thought of priming the carburetor with a little gasoline poured down its throat. But I didn't have a spare gas can. I rummaged for a hose but it proved too short to reach the low level of fuel in the Ford's tank.

We had passed a crew truck parked on the side of the road not far back, where the final day's planters had set out. Maybe someone was looking after us; maybe I hadn't picked a theology student for nothing. The question remained, however, whether the crew truck's gas tank was full enough to tap with my short length of hose.

I got on my knees and sucked until a rush of gasoline spurted into my mouth; I couldn't help swallowing some. I repeated the odious rite, more carefully this time, until enough gas dribbled through the hose to fill a small bottle.

The thirsty carburetor sputtered to life. Now we could drive on through several minor washouts to the eight-kilometer mark, where we were stopped by a raging river cutting through the road. On the other side an old shed lay on its side, victim to a previous spring flood.

Time to get out and walk...or swim. I hesitated, weighing what to do with the truck key. Should I leave it in the ignition so someone else could drive, in case something happened to us? Or so someone could steal it? Who? As a compromise, I left the doors unlocked but pocketed the key.

A slender poplar had been good enough to fall neatly across the torrent of runoff. Matt and I stripped off our boots and pants, heaved them across the creek, put our backpacks on, and waded across, using the poplar as a handy banister to brace ourselves against the frigid current. Then we dressed and walked on, in high spirits, down the last stretch of road, vast mountains towering up on both sides of the narrow valley.

Where the trail was supposed to start, an old cut-block rose above the road, partially logged, with a few old skid roads crisscrossing it and disappearing into the remaining growth of trees at the edges. I pulled out the dog-eared map that I'd drawn with directions from the forestry office to get our proper bearings. The map proved not to match the actual layout of skid roads on the site. After three-quarters of an hour of fruitless trial and error, we gave up and decided to follow our noses uphill in the general direction of the pass, which we could see from the clearing.

Wet from an overnight rain, the dense alder offered plenty of handholds. Matt and I put on our raingear and managed the ascent without much difficulty in a couple of hours of climbing, jumping creeks, crossing boulder fields, and snowslides. Then we picked our way along a precipitous rock face until we stood beneath the final, broad, steep approach to the pass itself.

Our destination hovered just beyond, a distant dream coming true. All around us was a profusion of alpine flowers, moss, and sparkling rivulets, and a mantle of shifting clouds over patches of ice and snow. I had to admire this grand view with the foul taste of gasoline burping up in my mouth.

We crawled like snails up the slick bank of compact mud and shale above the flowers. Our boots balanced by toe-tips on the slimmest of notches kicked into the hard surface, our fingers grasping at ephemeral stone chips that went skittering away at our touch. At last we arrived in the snowy pass, with its Christmas-card cabin nestled some two hundred meters away beside a half-frozen pond.

Nowick Gray

Chapter Five

Did I really expect to see Faron, Suze, and Ron all cozy in the cabin, drinking tea and smiling for us when we arrived? Returning from my scouting mission, I walked back into the cabin, stamping the snow off my boots, ready at least to warm up while waiting. Matt sat with his feet up, roasting by the stove, apparently unconcerned.

"No sign of them yet?"

"No."

He read my face, my heavy voice, and said, "I wouldn't panic about it. There's plenty of daylight left."

He looked the part of the preacher, with that smug assurance. I wasn't about to embark on a discussion with him about God's benevolent hidden agenda behind the world's disasters.

Anyway, he was not there to talk shop. "Before you take those boots off, how about we climb that hill behind the cabin for a better view of what's around us?"

We ascended the hill and scanned the awesome mountain peaks that ranged everywhere around us. To the west loomed blue-black, glacier-filled masses of raw granite. To the east rose the red-rock giants of the dryer, eastern flank of the range. Down the Grand Creek valley lay the lesser slopes we'd spent the last month planting. We studied our topographic maps, then sat still for a while to meditate on the desolate beauty of it all.

Finally, we slid down the icy slope and retired to the cabin for more tea and warming of hands by the woodstove. I hung up my wet clothes to dry and, clad in long johns and a sweater, sat down to wait. With the sun's rays slanting lower through the cabin's tiny west windows, I sat silent and reflective, brooding over the dubious wisdom of this so-called adventure. An hour had passed, still with no sign of Farah, Suze, and Ron.

Then I heard it—a voice calling in the

distance! I slipped on a pair of the cabin's battered old running shoes and ran out the door, down the rickety steps, and across the snow in the direction of the shouts. The voice grew louder, closer.

A series of little parallel ridges, spines of alpine rock, and scrub trees angled down from the cabin toward the headwaters of Tumbler Creek. Faron came into view a hundred meters away along one of the ridges, carrying a large backpack as well as Suze on her shoulders.

We approached with the gravitational force of our long-delayed closeness. Within reach, Faron's face beamed vibrantly under her bedraggled hair and skewed wool cap. We embraced in a long, strong silence.

Finally words came, breathless and trembling.

I said to Faron, "You made it."

"Yes. I can't believe we're finally together."

"You came alone? What about Ron?"

"When I drove by to pick him up, he said he was sick and couldn't make it."

"Oh, Faron. You look exhausted."

Suze still sat above me on Faron's

shoulders, bundled in her purple snowsuit. I picked her up into the air and then cuddled her joyfully.

"I walked some-a-way myself," the cherub proclaimed.

"For a long way," Faron added. "And she would have walked more, except she was so slow, I didn't want to take the time."

"I was getting worried. We've been here over an hour."

"What time is it?"

"Four-fifteen."

"Oh—we're practically right on time, then. It's only three-fifteen, our time."

For all my figuring of logistics, I'd forgotten we would be meeting on the time-zone boundary; I'd worried for nothing.

Faron had more to say about the difficulty of the way up. The trail she'd been following petered out in the alpine, and she'd come by instinct the last half-hour or so in the rough direction of the pass. Hiking up among the ridges on the west side, she lacked the clear line of sight that had guided us to the cabin from the east. Attaining the lower bowl of the pass, she'd lost her bearings and had to depend on her voice to make final contact with us.

***

When we arrived at the cabin, Faron exchanged brief greetings with Matt, unstrapped her pack, and collapsed on one of the bunks.

I helped Suze out of her snowsuit and boots. As I did so she said in a thin, shy voice, "Will, I'nt someping a-eat."

Parenting on a first-name basis, I remained a parent. "Okay, Suze, what would you like?"

"Someping from backpack."

I found Faron's pack crammed with extra warm clothes for two, bedding for three, food for a group, toys and books and art supplies for Suze, and a bundle of mail for me—at least thirty pounds, with Suze doubling the load.

"Faron, you didn't have to bring all this stuff, did you?"

"I thought you'd want to see those new books you ordered."

"Yeah, but I could have waited! I mean, I appreciate it, but all the way up here? And the junk mail—"

"It doesn't weigh that much."

I wasn't sure whether to admire her or

simply feel appalled at the extent of her ambitions. I sat beside her, putting my arm around her. She leaned her head against my shoulder. I could feel the weight of her exhaustion and relief. It was so good to see Faron, to hold her again like that.

Suze reminded me of my promise of food. I found her a muffin and sat back down beside Faron. I wanted nothing more than to cuddle with her under the bulky down comforter she'd brought along.

Matt graciously took his flute outside to serenade the mountains and left us to ourselves. Faron, chilled from her trek, kept her down coat on as we lay on the bunk in a tender embrace. That didn't matter; we could at last lie still, with mingled feelings of excitement, fatigue, accomplishment, and good fortune. By the time Matt returned, Faron had almost drifted into the mists of sleep.

***

After a supper of lentils and vegetables, rice cakes, fruit, and mixed nuts, we gathered around the cabin's logbook while a light rain fell outside. We learned that the shelter had withstood thirteen years of the clashing of weather systems at the top of this mountain range, where moist air traveling from the coast dropped its last load of rain and snow before reaching the Rockies. Entries in every month of the year recounted blizzards. We felt snug enough so far, though we had reason to be apprehensive as we closed the logbook and prepared for bed.

Matt chose one of the top bunks. I made Suze's bed under his, while Faron piled our comforter on the other bottom bunk. Outside, the wind was picking up. We put more wood in the fire for the night and dove, shivering, into our nests.

Love was never so lovely as this, so patiently earned; so forgiving of the weeks we'd spent apart, and those yet to come; so generous with its soothing balm. We tasted the fruition of our romantic quest. Our hands played over the rediscovered terrain of our skin, finding soft echoes of the mountains, rivers, and forests that lay all around us in the unseen night. The roar of our passion was muted out of respect for Matt's close-by solitude, and so transmuted into deeper frequencies, richer harmonies, more resounding exclamations of the heart.

The cabin walls shook with the buffeting of wind and rain, while thunder and lightning made a mounting attack on the darkness. Our bodies clung together into the night, courting sleep.

Somewhere in the realm between love and the void, we heard a crashing of wood outside. Faron's eyes popped open—I could feel the lashes against my cheek. In a flash I was alert to the arrival of a grizzly, come to claim the new food in its domain.

Or maybe it was the wind blowing boards about. As the sounds subsided amid the general cracking of the elements, the way opened to the dreamful night.

Chapter Six

I was in a hallway, a long, cockeyed room like a carnival crazy house: sloping floor, walls out of plumb, shadows painted at random along its indeterminate length. I walked slowly down (or was it up?) this narrow passage, noting the seven doors I passed, all closed. At the end I came to a warped mirror. I didn't like what I saw there: seven more doors, and a wobbly me, stretching backward and forward forever. At the end of the hall where I thought I'd started, I found another mirror, like the first. There was no exit now, I decided, except through one of the doors.

But which one? They all looked the same. Did they lead to different rooms, a common "outside"? Or to another hall, or halls, just like this one? I paced the length of that hall several times, deliberating. Nothing was changing: I would have to choose. Yes, I wanted to get out. I had to get out, that much I knew. Why, I didn't know. I would not stay in this oblong box.

I chose the first door—that is, the closest to an end of the hall. By now I couldn't remember which end it was, but it hardly mattered, as far as I could tell.

***

The morning light found Faron and me wrapped in one another's arms. Suze still slept, as did Matt, in the bunks farther down on the cabin wall. As our thoughts awakened in the soft light and softening wind, our limbs came alive once again to the exquisite touch of each other's skin, so tender, so transparent with feeling. We breathed together, our blood coursing as one, our loins throbbing to a rapid, then a slowing tempo. We lay for a long time looking into each other's luminous eyes.

Suze stirred and awoke. Her little cooing noises rose up into the chill air and brought further stirring from Matt's bunk. Faron and I still lay in reverent silence. Suze peeked her head around the partition between our bunks and came crawling into bed with us. Our arms wrapped around each other in delight.

All too soon, we plunged out of the covers and into cold clothes, amid cheery good mornings delivered with frosty breath. Matt and I briskly bustled about, making breakfast, while Faron dressed Suze and then started packing.

Breakfast was dried fruit, porridge, nuts, and leftover soup. We savored it as a feast. I knew from Faron's glowing silence that she still bathed with me in the wonder of our renewed connection. Matt and even Suze seemed also to be chewing in a reflective spirit, honoring the occasion.

Then there was time only to write our regards to the cabin and the mountains in the logbook, stuff our packs full once again, and head off to our separate destinations. I accompanied Faron, with Suze on my shoulders, to the end of the top ridge, where their descent would begin.

We stood there holding one another for many long, blissful moments in a gray, icy drizzle, saying good-bye, our wet cheeks pressed warmly together. With visibility no more than three feet, I was sending my family into the void. The final bliss of our parting now became painful. They vanished into the mists, and I trudged back to the cabin to begin my own descent on the other side of the mountain.

***

As I entered the cabin door, I discovered with some horror that I was back in that oblong, misshapen hallway. Quickly I groped behind me to get back out, but the door was shut now, and when I whirled to try it with all my strength, I found it locked.

Very well, then, I can accept what fate throws my way; I'll choose another—if one may be found still unlocked. I strode to the far end of the hallway, gave myself a crooked smile of assumed confidence, and opened the door.

Chapter Seven

We awoke in the morning light, clinging together. Faron was turned to face outward, and I, with the wall to my back, wrapped my arms around her from behind. Matt stirred from the upper bunk farther along the wall.

He crowed, "Good morning, Faron. And Will."

Faron took a deep breath; too deep. "Good…morning."

"Hi," I said.

"Did you sleep well?" Matt had turned and stretched half out of bed toward us, looking at Faron.

"Not too bad," she replied, "except for that crashing outside. I thought a bear might be trying to get in."

"Yeah, me too," I chimed in.

"It must have been the old wood scraps blowing around," said Matt. "Hey, who's on breakfast?"

Faron turned to look at me, a silent query.

"Oh, I don't mind," I volunteered.

"No, I was kidding," said Matt. "I'd be glad to do it." And with that, his long muscular body jumped out of bed, stark naked, onto the floor in front of Faron. She shrank back involuntarily at the sight, but kept facing him. Matt took pains to find the right clothing for the day's descent before putting anything on.

My own thin arms felt dead now around Faron's waist. She moved away, out of the covers and onto the floor, and bounced up and down in the cold air.

"Brrrr!" she blurted out, as Matt scanned the bounty of her body with admiring eyes. "Now let's see. What warm clothes can I wear today?" Her ample breasts jounced and swayed as she grabbed for her clothes.

Matt was taking his time with his own clothes, I noticed, as the show went on. Faron's legs were openly displayed as she stepped into her pants.

I turned my back on both these burlesque actors and stared at the wall, breathing deeply. Suze poked her head around the partition between our bunks. Her cupid's head sported an impish grin.

"Look, Faron, Matt has pee-nee!"

It had just flopped into his underpants as he tugged them on. Faron laughed.

I looked at her sharply. She scowled back at me, zipping her own pants tight.

"Faron, did you see it?" the tyke persisted. "It can give you babies."

Now Matt blushed. I waited for Faron to set the record straight. Finally I couldn't stand the silence. "Come on, Suze," I said, jumping out of bed in my long johns and picking her up. "Let's get you dressed. Are you hungry?"

Matt seemed to have lost interest in clothing himself any further as he turned to the job of packing. I finished dressing Suze and myself and started on breakfast. I lit the wood stove, cranked up the Coleman to boil water for porridge, and ventured outside for more water from the pond.

My mind raced over images of the previous evening, trying to recall evidence of the apparent attraction between my wife—well, common law, anyway—and this friend—well, recent acquaintance. I found nothing to put my finger on...until I remembered Matt's off-color story about the guy in the hot tub at Columbiana who'd said the tubs didn't have wood liners because there would be too many orgasms—er, organisms. Oh, how Faron had laughed, as if she were having one right on the spot.

Faron and I had been together just four years. *How deep is her loyalty to me?* I wondered. Well, Christ, there was the child, at least, to think about.

I dipped the bucket in the pond, trying to divine in that cold pool what I might see when I got back to the cabin. Faron and Matt hugging—an innocent, friendly, warming hug, I tried to tell myself. In the steel-cold water they lingered in their embrace, for me to see as I crossed their threshold; Matt still shirtless, Faron flushed red.

We would eat a desultory breakfast together. Then Faron's question would come: "When will we see you again, Matt?"

He would, of course, be delighted to

answer: "As a matter of fact, I've been hoping to get to Homewood ever since Will told me about where you live. It sounds like a pretty neat place. As for my plans—well, they've changed a bit, recently. I was going to go back to Vancouver with my friend Janet, but now her plans have changed, too, and she's going back alone. So maybe I will have a couple of weeks to spare...."

And so it would go. Faron's inevitable response ("Oh, you should come stay with us for a while, and have a long enough visit so we can really get to know each other") was practically audible to my burning ears as I mounted the steps with the sloshing bucket, wondering whether I should knock first. I heard the sound of quick, shuffling bodies inside. I opened the door....

Chapter Eight

Of course. Back home again, jiggedy-jig. Whoever was responsible for this cruel joke, I was not amused. The combination of lentils and fruit? I tossed and turned. Boards banged; the little room rocked from side to side—walls shifting, floorboards groaning. Invisible windows threw blackness back into itself. I considered getting up and going outside again, this time to investigate that infernal banging. But I couldn't even see the door in the dark.

Then lightning flashed. The room reeled eerily. A door became visible for an instant. I almost awoke enough to make the effort. Then, I could see a row of doors, at least three to choose from.

I chose the middle door, and as I walked

through, it shut behind me like a trap.

***

Matt and I stood not five minutes down the mud-and-shale bank just below the pass, looking at the ground. The bear shit steamed in the cold morning mist, just at the point where the flowers began.

Our progress had come to a chilly halt at the fresh sign. Our eyes swept the landscape, near and far. No bears. I wondered what this grizz had eaten, and how recently. It owned this mountain ridge, sniffing and browsing every inch of it.

Which would be worse? was my paranoid query as I followed Matt's lead, creeping down the slope. For a bear to kill Faron and Suze, leaving me without them? Or for the bear to snap me in half like so much dry spaghetti, leaving them to grieve? Maybe, I dared to hope, our love, so fresh and strong, would keep the bear away.

But no. We could hear the giant just below us, in the boulder slide, large rocks knocking together, with upwards of a thousand pounds of grizzly tipping the balance. We saw the animal at the same time as it turned its head up to us; it snorted with a loud "HWMFF."

Sweat broke out on my neck. Matt gaped up at me with an instantaneous look of fright. It was the first time I'd seen anything but confidence in him. He was experienced, all right; and seeing this bear's behavior, his eyes softened with what I perceived as the gentle acceptance of the saint.

The bear charged. It leaped up the hill, practically flying with its enormous bulk over the boulders and onto the adjoining mud-and-shale slide. Matt, crouching closest, knew to drop to the ground, clutching his head in his curled arms and squeezing his knees up against his vulnerable belly.

Ursus horribilis pounced on him in an instant, growling and whoofing, cuffing him with its huge paws. The stiletto-like claws tore Matt's vest to ribbons. The escaping down floated around them both like a cloud of tiny angels.

This flurry seemed to amuse, then infuriate the bear. It first sat back on its haunches, waiting for the feather storm to subside—and while doing so, stole a quick look at me, frozen up the bank twenty human paces away. Then, with the quickness of a rattlesnake, the bear's muzzle clamped shut on Matt's neck. The severed jugular spouted all over the cursed place; Matt's poor waste of a body was left to flop about like a beached fish.

The bear stepped back until the death throes were complete, then it nosed forward to lap up a taste of the blood. Faint from the shock of what I had just witnessed, and what I feared was in store for me, I lay on the ground immobile, knowing there was nothing I could do. No more choices, no more plans…nothing more to worry about going wrong on this so-called adventure. No more rendezvous with Faron and Suze, nor Harris and the gang, nor anyone but Dr. D.

Then the beast, already bored with its lifeless prey, turned its glittering eyes and red mouth my way.

***

I awoke with a start, my throat constricted with a strangled cry from deep within the darkness. As the morning dawned through thick fog, sporadic gusts of wind still blew scattered rain against the roof and walls.

All right, I thought to myself. *It's all right;*

I didn't even come back here through any goddamned door—at least, not that I remember.

Faron may have still been asleep, but I hugged her so tightly she woke up, turned to face me, and smiled. Then I leaned out of bed to peek at Suze. She lay neatly tucked in her bed, peaceful as an angel, her rosebud mouth relaxed, her eyelashes so delicate as they lightly lay on her downy, cream-colored cheeks. Then quite suddenly, her eyes opened and blinked several times.

"I have a bad dream."

"Oh," I said. "I'm sorry to hear that. Do you want to tell me about it?"

"No-ey. Was too scary. Will, we are gonna go home today?"

"Yes. Except, Suze, you know what?"

"What?"

"You and Faron are going down one side of the mountain, and Matt and I are going down the other."

"Oh, but…then I want to go tree pranting wif you."

"That would be nice, Suze, but you can't. I need to make lots of money so we can buy things we need, like food for you, and gas for the truck."

"Oh."

"Besides, you'll be with Faron."

"Yeah," she said, with a strange little darkness crossing her brow. "But Will, Faron might miss you, too."

"Yes," I said. "And I'll miss Faron, and you too."

Then we had breakfast to fix, and backpacks to stuff; jobs to return to. Before I knew it our little vacation had come to an end, and I was following Faron and poor little Suze out the cabin door.

***

The night was long and wild. The wind carried me along in the clouds. There were deer dancing in the stars that I couldn't see. They peeked their heads down through the clouds to say hello, then went back to their dancing.

Bears were everywhere, looking for food, but also hiding behind corners, rocks, low clumps of trees. I thought this was where, in the wintertime, Santa Claus lived.

When it got light in the morning the deer rode away on the stars, and the bears all disappeared, and I woke up. Faron and Will woke up, too. And Matt. They got me dressed, and we ate porridge and soup and nuts. Soup for breakfast! Leftovers, goo-guk. They let me have figs to eat when we started to walk down the mountain. I was cold. There was snow on the ground. I was wearing my purple snowsuit, but it was raining in the sky and my snowsuit got all wet. My face was wet like tears all over it—but I didn't cry, not even when Will and Matt left me and Faron to walk home by ourself.

Faron carried me a long, long way. She said we were walking in the clouds, just like an airplane, or geese. But an airplane doesn't walk, silly.

I flapped my arms. We flew down the mountain. I was cold and wanted to go to sleep in the black truck. Faron was tired and wanted me to walk. I was too tired. I cried when she put me down on the ground. We rested and ate some nuts that I held in my hand. But I dropped some, my fingers were so cold.

The bears could eat them, I thought.

Do bears eat people?

Faron said not usually. I wanted to go back

up on her shoulders.

We finally got to the black truck. I woke up when Faron strapped me in my kid-seat. I looked out the window and the bears and the deer were saying good-bye. But I didn't wave. I didn't want them to see my eyes.

Then we drove away, down the bumpy road. Va, va; ya, ya, ya. I was hungry again, but Faron said I would have to wait. I started to complain, and Faron said stop complaining, she had to drive; but I was so hungry, and still cold, and I started to cry. Then we were going so slow, I thought we would stop and she would feed me.

Faron said she was just trying to be careful; I had to wait. I stopped crying and said blow my nose, Faron.

Just wait, she said, mad at me. I don't know why she got so mad at me. Then—

The truck fell over. And over, and over and over, down the hill, we fell off the road, down the hill and the truck was flying, like an airplane but upside down, and it was quiet like in the clouds.

Then we bumped down so hard! And the roof was all crunched in, and I could see

Faron's head broken and I screamed—

***

I lost it—thanks to those strings pulled by the watchful mind. The good strings, and the not so good. I'm glad that the curtains are on auto-drop when the scene goes to absolute hell.

Or was it I who got the drop, through some infernal trap door that left me, far from salvation, lost in the center of a maze? What I saw was simple enough: an oblong box, irregular of construction—or misshapen from weathering, or warped by some trick played by the conspiracy of eye and mind, mirror and eye, mirror and mirror....

Still the row of doors; I couldn't remember which I'd tried, so I tried them all, turning the knobs to see which I might yet open, just to get my options clear. So I could put all my rational faculties to best use.

Through each cracked-open door, I heard a distant sound of hollow laughter, and the skin crawled briefly up my back. Four doors locked. Could I assume these represented my choices thus far? I could assume nothing. But that was my hypothesis, for better or worse. And so I had but three remaining doors to try. I was beginning to wonder if there was any point to guesswork, or if this was a setup to run me through the mill before the final door. And then—what?

I blindly grabbed the nearest knob and it came off in my hand. In a rage I flung it at the mirror at the far end of the hall, where it created a shattering explosion of shards. One small but deeply seated sliver I had to remove from my own wrist. And then, with blood on my hands, I boldly marched through the swaying door without so much as a peek through the doorknob's empty hole.

Chapter Nine

Morning dawned through misty, drizzling sleet. Visibility, if you chose to call it that, was practically nil as we got up and peered out the cabin windows. We dressed for wet weather and packed up the rest of our things. Matt fetched some water from the pond for the porridge pot, shaking the sleet and wet snow from his hair and boots when he came back in. We sat down on folding chairs at the table, mulling over the prospects before us. Faron held Suze on her lap.

"What's it going to be like finding your trail?" I asked Faron.

She took a large breath. "Oh, I don't know. I guess I'll find out when I get there."

Matt had a suggestion. "Maybe, Will, you

could go partway down with them, until Faron gets started on the trail. Or I could come too if you want, and help with the load."

Good basic idea, I thought; but there were other factors to consider. I looked at my watch. "Gee, I don't know. Would we have enough time left to get to Columbiana for our four-thirty phone call? If we miss the guy in the company office, we won't know where the new camp is, and we'll miss work tomorrow. Also, isn't Harris going to send help looking for us if we don't show up tonight?"

"They might start worrying. But really, it shouldn't take us more than two hours to get to the road, then another hour's walk to the truck."

"Okay," I said. "Let's say five hours to Columbiana, to be safe. It's after nine now. If we left right away, that would give us no more than an hour to go down with them on their side, another hour to come back here. And we still have to get on coats, and boots, and Suze's things."

Faron spoke up now. "I think I'll be fine. I made it okay carrying everything uphill. Maybe, Will, you could walk down with us just to where we met you on our way up."

Somehow I knew that Faron's self-reliance would assert itself here. I readily agreed to this plan. Now I could be helpful to her, and we could say our little family farewell alone together out in the wild and whirling elements, without jeopardizing my schedule.

"I'll stay and finish cleaning up," said Matt, deferring to our decision. "Then we'll be ready to go when you get back."

***

Ten minutes out of the cabin, we were all three soaking wet. Faron's down coat and Suze's polyester were slick with the freezing rain; Faron's hair streamed out from under the edges of her soggy wool hat; and both their faces gleamed with the shiny glow of the exercise and the glaze of sleet. We couldn't see very much at all...traces of footprints here and there in the patchy snow along the ridged rock...white air.

We followed our noses some ten minutes further, and then I turned the backpack over to Faron. She looked around uncertainly, trying vainly to recognize some landmark or sign of her passage the day before. We were now past any leftover footprints, and visibility remained negligible. I tried to offer some final guidance before turning them loose.

"We know Bastille's over that way. So down there a little farther to the right, that deep draw goes down toward Tumbler Creek, and then your trail must be somewhere farther right, pretty much downhill from here."

"Yeah, I guess so. But it comes straight up the hill a long way from where it follows the contour. If I don't find where it starts up high, I'm not likely to find it until way down below."

"Well," I persisted, conscious of time ticking away, "we lost the trail on our side and just bushwhacked uphill. And I guess we'll do the same on the way down. If you just head straight down you're bound to end up on the trail eventually—or if not, you'll come out on the road, or down to Tumbler Creek itself. Either way you'll know where you are."

Faron still seemed uncertain. "I did tell Ron that if I wasn't back by seven he was to come out looking for me." She looked intently into the white haze. "This ridge here looks kind of familiar," she ventured, putting on a bright face.

"Are you sure you'll be okay now? I could still come down with you part way, a little more, if I would be any help—"

But by now I already knew that her mind was made up.

"No, that's okay. We'll be all right, thanks."

We stood and held each other close, our cool cheeks firmly pressed together against the sleet, for a long moment meant to last until another reunion—another time and place, home.

I left them and turned back up the ridge to the cabin. When I looked back, Faron and Suze were gone into the clouds below.

***

I had a strange feeling of uneasy hesitation as I opened the cabin door—was it a premonition of some disaster, a bad decision, a wrong turn on the forked road of this fragile labyrinth we call life? I turned and gazed off into the vague and formless western sky. Was it too late to go back and help them find the trail? My hand still clutched the latch of the cabin door. Yes, too late. I would go on ahead, and trust that it would be all right in the end.

The packs stood ready by the bunks, and Matt was putting plates and bowls away. I thanked him for doing the dishes.

"Oh, no problem," he said. "How'd it go? Did you manage to find the trail?"

"Oh, no problem," I wished I could echo. *Maybe*, I thought, *Matt should have come along with us after all.* I told him the truth. "Not exactly. But I think we got to the right general area. Faron said it looked familiar."

Matt looked dubious. He didn't know what to say. I told him what I'd told Faron, that if necessary she could head straight downhill.

"Yeah, that makes sense," he said, nodding slightly. "I guess so, anyway. If you thought they were going to be okay...." His voice trailed off, and his eyes fell to the floor. He turned to the packs. "We'd better get going ourselves then, eh?"

***

Within minutes down the east side from the pass, the air was clearer and drier. Evidently the foul weather was expending itself against the western bulwark of the pass and the adjoining ridges that formed the height of land along the spine of the Purcell cordillera.

Matt commented about Faron's strength and courage; I bathed in the glow of appreciation and respect for her. And I hoped that the trip had been worth the effort for Matt, who hadn't enjoyed the rewards I had.

The ground was still slick and slippery, but once we'd picked our way down the mud-and-shale slope just below the pass, we could walk in fairly full stride.

We reached the truck with time to spare, and drove on past Columbiana into Inverness. It was still only four o'clock when I phoned the company office for directions to the new camp location. Then I phoned Faron.

No answer. Still perhaps too early. Her descent was about the same distance as ours, with a similar drive to get home from the foot of the trail. But she was no doubt slower with her extra-heavy load.

Matt and I decided to stay for an early but much-needed supper in Inverness. I was worried. We talked about what we could have done but didn't—because I was so concerned about earning an extra day's wages...wagering two lives, my life, for a hundred dollars. We agreed that Faron had likely had trouble finding the trail, and Matt reminded me of the obvious; that she would have taken extra time to find it.

Still, I hardly tasted my lasagna. Matt ate fish and chips with similar disinterest. He was concerned about hypothermia if they strayed across the mountainside too long, especially under the threat of coming darkness. I phoned again right after supper. Still no answer.

***

The next stop was Belford, two and a half hours away on the highway toward Carston. The rest of the crew had ended up booking a ski-lodge called the Purcell Condo. Plans had changed slightly. No more propane showers that ran fire-and-ice; now we could relax after work with whirlpool hot tubs and color TV. There was a pay phone in the lobby.

Matt went to check in with Harris. I phoned home again and once more got no answer. After eight o'clock already; it would be dark in another hour. *Surely*, I thought, *Faron should have been back home by six or seven.* Maybe she had stopped at Ron's on the way home and got invited for supper.

I phoned Ron's place. No answer there, either, so I tried Faron's sister and close neighbor, Sandra. She told me Faron hadn't been heard from, and that Ron had phoned a half an hour ago to say he was organizing a search party. They would head up to Tumbler Creek right away. By now they had probably left.

I said I'd drive on around to meet them and join the search. Sandra started to tell me not to worry, but my voice started to choke as I thanked her and quickly hung up.

Matt had vanished down the faceless corridors, the neat rows of nameless doors standing innocently at attention (one of them reserved for me). I knew Matt would be concerned and would likely want to come with me, but I wasn't about to start knocking on doors to look for him now. I was out the big glass doors of the lobby and on the road. Let them figure out where I'd gone.

***

As I stopped in town first for gas and a thermos of coffee, I considered the futility of an after-dark search. Yet something had to be done; Faron and Suze couldn't be left out there in weather like that. If they were conscious and lost, the search party might locate them by voice. Yes, it was definitely worth trying, in nighttime hours that might otherwise see them go over into irreversible darkness.

I barreled down the highway, trying to imagine what could have happened. I blamed myself, of course, because it would have been so easy to go down with them to the trail. And now? Maybe Faron had turned an ankle and just needed to sit tight and stay warm until help arrived. Or maybe a bear...I put that thought out of my mind. No, she must have simply lost her bearings and wandered through the sleet and fog, both their coats soaking through to the skin, Suze stoic with the cold rain streaming down her cheeks as the tears would if she hadn't been holding them back, in her blind trust in Faron to lead them back to the truck and home.

I pictured Faron trying, with increasing desperation, to guess which way to go, whether to veer left or right. If she headed too far left, she stood the chance of bypassing the rise of the trail altogether and ending up in the untracked vastness beneath the glaciers. So probably, she would angle to the right. But that way she might also miss the upper trail, and would end up instead high above its lower contour, separated from it by hundreds of feet of steep, slippery brush. So she'd have to backtrack, and by then she'd be exhausted from trying to keep her footing on the alder stems that covered the ground like millions of greased rails—not to mention the sixty pounds of load taking its toll on her shoulders, leg, back, and spirit. Suze's patience, meanwhile, would have surely worn thin and given way to moans and whimpers. If Faron had considered making the child walk, now she would realize that under such conditions, that would be even worse than carrying her.

So Faron would perhaps consider an attempt to return to the cabin in the pass. Her pride and determination to forge ahead would be a force against such an option—as would the prospect of hiking back uphill still lost, ever more fatigued, with darkness fast approaching.

In fact, the night was fully upon us by now, and for a while on the road my mind was as blank and black as sky and coffee coursing toward dawn. It was three-thirty when I hit the turnoff to home, and with impulsive hope I decided to drive in as far as Ron's house to see if they were back. But his car was gone, and the house, as I peeked and called inside the front door, was empty.

***

Back on the road up to Tumbler Creek, my heart sank to a new and frightening depth. I could envision it all. The trucks parked at the bottom of the trail. Me heading up in the early light, suddenly alert and energetic, shouting as I go. The blinding glare of fresh snow on the ground. An answering shout, muffled by snow and distance, way off to the left, off the trail that continues up and to the right. Scrambling across the contour, through the upper reaches of alder, the patches of juniper shrub, and walls of slick shale. The repeated calls coming at me from a slightly higher elevation as I cross.

"We found her," I finally hear—and the way I hear it, it doesn't sound encouraging.

Then, I see Ron bent over Faron's still form, blowing air into her mouth. Useless.

Suze, somewhere else, downhill. Cold, useless.

How? (*Why* is too painful, full of me.) How?

***

Sometime later, entering my empty house at home, my living tomb, I see in the darkness:

70

Faron, trembling with exhaustion, hefting Suze off her shoulders and down onto the ground. The child waiting while the backpack is discarded. A startled cry, and Faron turning to see our daughter rolling down the hill like a tumbleweed.

A scream from Faron—Suze is strangely silent now, still rolling away out of sight through the wet alder. Faron jumps up, slips back to the ground and scrambles on her stomach, knees and elbows, grappling holds with numb hands on slick roots....

Her foot catches on a root and she, too, tumbles head over heels, but her head comes down on the first roll against a large, round rock.

When she wakes up, the rain has stopped. Suze is gone. Faron can't move, but realizes, gradually, that that's okay. Then she feels a breath on her neck and turns to find Suze, warm and dry as a newly bathed and powdered babe, snuggling in her original nakedness up to her own naked body. The two of them lie in the spring flowers, the sunshine relaxing their pale, supple flesh into one, with the milk and breath and blood flowing between them again…mother and child.

Chapter Ten

Now I see; this is my house. I've tried all the doors but two. By now, I've seen it all. What can be worse? I walk like a condemned man through the next to last doorway, noticing at the last moment that the door beside it is cracked and weathered, and wears a handle instead of a knob; but that's all right, one circle of hell's as much damned fun as the next.

***

It was a fearful night. As morning dawned through thick fog, sporadic gusts of wind still blew scattered rain against the roof and walls. When I finally got up and went outside to pee, I shivered in the icy drizzle on my hair and bare arms, and shuddered back inside as quickly as I could.

Faron was sitting up looking out the window. "I don't know how I'm going to find the trail like this."

"You mean naked? You'd better dress warmly, then." I hurried back onto the bunk and draped my arms around her.

"No, silly…." She turned her head and smiled briefly, brushing a kiss against my shoulder. "I'm serious. I mean, it was hard enough to follow the trail on the way up when I could see. This is ridiculous."

Matt poked his head down from his bunk. "Good morning—such as it is."

"What do you think?" I asked him.

"Well, it looks like a mess out there all right. But it's likely to be clearer as we get farther down in elevation."

"What about Faron's trail, which she lost even on the way up?"

"I don't know. Maybe we should go with her till we find it."

"Yeah, that makes sense." I gave Faron a little squeeze with my long, bare arms; she still held the bedclothes in front of her. I said to her, "Matt and I could leave our packs back at the cabin, and we could help you carry Suze and your backpack at least part of the way down."

Faron was still dubious. "What if you guys got lost on the way back? You wouldn't even have your packs."

Matt and I discussed briefly the problem of timing...whether we could make it down the east side for our four-thirty phone call. It seemed it could work if all went well.

Faron turned to the window again. "Now it's snowing."

Large, soft flakes streamed down in a spontaneous blizzard.

I quickened the pace: "We should eat and run, then, if we're going ahead with our plan, before it gets too bad out there."

"Yeah," Suze chimed in. "Eat and run!"

***

By the time Matt returned from washing dishes at the pond, he could report that the fresh snow was an inch deep. He couldn't see the cabin from the pond, and could barely follow his own tracks back.

When Faron heard that, she stopped packing. "Goodness. I don't know about this. With all that snow on the trail, maybe we should wait. It's bound to melt...." She looked unhopefully out the window again.

"Or get deeper," I added. "It's not as if we had a week's food supply here. We should decide pretty quick if we're going at all."

Again we tossed around our options...the jobs to return to, the people waiting for us below on both sides of the pass. The idea of a search party (or two), mobilized into action on our behalf, while we sat there deliberating, made me wince, not to mention a day's wages lost. But outside, the snow fell faster and faster. It was almost a relief to watch it happening, making the decision clearer.

"We've got to think about first things first," I said to Faron finally. "Let's wait. It might just blow over."

Matt nodded. "I think that's a good idea."

Faron let out a loud sigh. "All right." It wasn't her usual style to let caution hold her back, but in this case her motherly intuition seemed to have gained the upper hand. She looked at Suze, who had been silently soaking it all in like a sponge. "Suze, we can unpack all your toys and books and crayons and coloring books, after all. We're going to stay here for a while until the snow stops and we can see where we're going."

***

The snow continued to fall. We read books, drank tea and cocoa, told our life histories, and philosophized about the ecumenical movement. Suze colored and played quietly, listening. Before the day was done, we'd read all her books to her half a dozen times; outside the snow was a foot deep. There was no sign of clearing as darkness fell.

Our food supplies were running thin. Suze had eaten the last rice cake in mid-afternoon. The soup and porridge were gone. We still had a handful of nuts and dried fruit left, which we'd been hoping to save for the hike down. The cupboard shelves had a little rice, maybe a cup. There was powdered milk, some more of the crusty old cocoa, a can of ox-tail soup. We decided on soup and rice for supper, with our trail food and cocoa scheduled for the next morning.

We ate in moody reflection of our fate that evening. The snowfall had lessened, I thought, as I trudged out to the pond to wash dishes. But I couldn't say for sure.

Faron and I colored with Suze while Matt

occupied himself with the logbook. When darkness fell we all crawled into our bunks once again. Matt was still absorbed in reading the logbook and took it to bed with a candle. Faron and I did not make love that night—we simply held each other close and still, until our bodies softened as one into sleep. Outside, the snow fell down and down, thicker and faster in the chill of the night.

***

Back in the box, I sat tight, cross-legged, on the slanting hallway floor: a sit-down strike. I refused to go through any doors. *Hell, they're probably all locked now anyway. But I won't give them the satisfaction.* Not that they, the stupid doors, cared. They were only the middlemen, the arch observers as I passed through them, or passed them by. *Let them wait, now, and see what happens.*

***

We got up, the usual scene in the cabin. Ate breakfast and packed to leave. Decided again to let Faron and Suze go down the mountainside—blind as bats, all of us. Matt and I down our side, past bear-sign, all the way to the road in a jaunty hour and a half, and on to the truck, cocky as all get out. Philosophizing about the role of religion in the modern world, for God's sake...comparing Christian prayer and Buddhist meditation, for instance, and their different approaches for the relief of suffering souls. We weren't suffering, by Jesus; we'd just made it up and back, adventure accomplished.

Only one problem. When we got in the truck and headed back towards Columbiana, we were stopped by a raging river where a nondescript little stream had crossed the road the day before. There was, in fact, no road left at all over a good ten-foot span.

Matt and I couldn't believe it. We paced back and forth, wondering what we'd done to bring such a fate down on our charmed heads, and what we were going to do about it. Especially me, because it was my truck and I hated to simply abandon it—or worse, to try a crossing and botch it, leaving the truck stranded for who knew how long.

I decided to risk it. With a good head of steam, and the high clearance of the heavy-duty frame, I thought we just might make it. I got in the truck, trying to radiate confidence. Matt hesitated only a second and then got in beside me to add his confidence, or the semblance of it, and I gunned the truck for all it was worth. The rear wheels churned and bucked over the river rock as we swayed halfway through the two-foot deep, rushing water. Then the engine sputtered, gasped, and died.

I looked at Matt, both our faces fallen. The truck, already unbalanced, tipped in a surge of current, then rolled over onto the passenger side. I pushed my door up into the air and clambered out, with Matt, all arms and legs, on my heels. We would have to jump into the middle of the stream. I had no footing when I hit bottom, and my legs were swept out from under me by the current rushing under the submerged side of the truck.

One leg got stuck under the truck and I struggled to keep my head out of the water. Matt crouched halfway out the upended driver's side, holding the door open with one hand and reaching for me with the other. Our fingertips stretched inches apart.

He had to come farther out of the truck to reach the bottom, so he propped the door open on its stiff hinge, and while holding onto the floor of the cab, extended his long legs down into the water. When he got his footing he reached down again to help me up, still holding onto the truck for support. As his firm right hand closed around my upraised elbow and pulled, the truck rocked slightly with the weight. The door gave out a sickening crack and swung down before I could yell, "Look out!" It smacked down hard on Matt's left hand. He screamed and let go of me. The current knocked me over again. I gulped water, realized my ankle had come free, got back to my knees, and finally to my feet. I grasped the handle of the truck door and opened it so Matt could pull out his hand.

"Fucking God," he said.

It showed only a small gash; he plunged it into cold water to ease the pain and swelling.

He stood leaning over, moaning; I stood soaked and shivering beside him. He felt the bones and said nothing was broken. I shifted weight to test my ankle; sore but intact.

"Fucking God," I quoted him. We stood there for a moment, and both of us gave way to tears of laughter, full of salvation and futility.

***

When the next day came, the weather had

not let up. Despite whatever unseen dangers lurked in wait for us on the way home, I awoke with the queasy feeling that we'd made a mistake in staying there, cooped up in that little box.

The cabin was still shrouded in thick fog, but there was one positive sign—the snow was coming down wetter. If we could just get down from the higher elevation, we'd be home free. If not, there would certainly be a search party, at least from the Homewood side, arriving soon. We figured it was safe to eat up the last of our nuts and dried fruit, along with the last of the cocoa and powdered milk, for breakfast.

We sat on our bunks eating silently. When that meager ration was gone, we found that our certainty too was eaten away. The popular subject of our fate was up for discussion again.

Faron remained cautious. I favored trying to get her and Suze started down on that trail. "What do you think?" I asked Matt.

"I think we should just stoke up this stove," he said, getting up to do just that, "and sit tight until this weather clears a bit. It's bound to change before too long, I bet by this afternoon. Then if no one's arrived from below, we could head down to find the trail, like you say."

"That would leave us too short of time for going down our side today, wouldn't it?"

"Depends. We might still have time. If it was before four or five, say, we'd be okay."

The fire roared now. We all edged a bit closer. Faron finally stood up and stationed herself next to the stove, warming her back.

"That sounds like a good plan to me," she said after some deliberation.

"Yeah, okay," I agreed.

"Oh, but I'm hungry," said Suze. "Faron, I want someping a-eat."

Faron twisted uncomfortably, looking as if she wished she hadn't heard that. "You'll have to wait, Suze. We'll go home later today, and you can have whatever you want to eat when we get home."

"And Suze, you just had breakfast," I added. "Besides, that was the last of our food."

"Oh, but how long will it be? I can't wait that long. I need someping a-eat. I need someping nowww." And she began to cry.

I offered to read her a favorite book, *The Three Little Pigs*. She forgot her hunger momentarily. Three books later, I needed a break, something to relieve my own boredom, to take my mind off my own hunger.

"Where's that logbook?" I asked Matt.

"It's still up by my bunk, on the windowsill," he told me. "Do you want me to get it down for you?"

"No, that's okay, I'll get it."

The little windowsill on the end wall of the cabin was beyond my reach, so I hefted myself up to the bunk, resting my knees there while I found the logbook. Then I jumped down onto the floor.

My right leg crunched through the thin plywood flooring, in a place I should have remembered was less than solid. I yelled in agony, and in distress at my stupidity. The left leg had held, over a joist; the right foot had twisted, half-catching the joist on its way through. It now felt broken, dangling in cold air.

Matt and Faron helped me out of the hole and examined the leg as I lay groaning on the floor with the stabbing pain. The foot was skewed at an unnatural angle, already purple and swollen.

Suze screeched as if taking my pain. I

soothed us both by holding her against my chest as I lay on the floor. When her panicked cries had quieted down to a soft, plaintive whimpering, Matt said he thought I should have a splint.

I didn't relish the prospect of forcing the bone straight again. Without really considering the alternative, I asked Matt, "Is is really necessary?"

"You'd be better off with it. With your leg loose, it would be too easy for the broken bone to tear through the skin. A splint will keep it stable. It may even start it healing properly."

"What will we need?" Faron asked him. "A board, some strips of cloth?"

"Yeah," said Matt. "Actually, a couple of boards, and some padding; I'll see what I can find outside."

Suze was now fascinated with the preparations. I could only think of the pain, and the pain to come. When the plank ends, strips of a T-shirt, and handfuls of melting moss were gathered at my feet, Matt bent to do his duty. Faron, holding Suze, knelt close beside me.

"This is probably going to hurt," Matt didn't need to say. I squeezed Faron's hand. He pulled gently, pushed slightly. Nothing happened; I lived. He tried again, harder, and this time I thought I was going to die. One attempt more, and bone cleared bone, sending a bolt of lightning straight through my head. But the ankle was almost straight. "I think that's going to have to do for now," my doctor decreed; and with Faron's help, he proceeded to wrap up half my leg, cushioned with moss pads, between the boards.

I managed to say, in a hoarse whisper, "Thanks, Matt."

He shrugged. "You know, I've never done that before, except on a dummy in a first-aid course years ago. It's not the same."

Faron bent closer and brushed her cheek against my suffering face. Her tears started flowing freely. I put my arms around her and let my own tears come. Then Suze, of course, also started crying, and Faron had to laugh and turn her attention to comforting the child.

"Are you ready to get off that hard floor, yet?" Matt asked. "You don't need a body splint, you know."

They helped me onto the lower bunk where Suze had slept. And then it was time to decide in earnest what to do. The snowfall had diminished, the sky shone a little brighter.

***

Faron and Suze headed down together to get help, hoping they'd meet a rescue party on their way. Matt and I spent the rest of the day waiting, helplessly waiting. The pain in my leg was unbearable, but I had to bear it. We had not even any tea left for Matt to nurse me with, never mind brandy, aspirin, morphine— anything to muffle the ringing, throbbing pain.

He tried to comfort me with thoughts of home, the approaching rescue, my deliverance from the hells of tree planting. He tried to divert us from our nagging, ever-present hunger with talk about baseball, politics, and the down-sliding economy. Faron hadn't returned, so she must have found the trail, unless she'd gotten lost. Or had got down to the bottom and then driven off the road. Or some other nameless possibility. The question remained: Where was that goddamned search party?

Suppertime came and went, providing no supper. I tried to read myself to sleep, without success.

The night was a dark and hostile place

whose walls leaned in and threatened to crush me, then fell back away so my body could lay open to cold, penetrating points of starlight.

***

In the morning we saw patches of blue sky beyond the billowing clouds of mist that still swept over the mountains. We felt certain it would be our last day there. But the clouds hung on, and by noon, when no help had arrived, Matt's patience had run out.

He'd just brought in a fresh load of firewood and dumped it in the box beside the stove, and now he stood between me and the door, with the door still open. His dark eyes sagged and his mouth was drawn down into his shaggy, black beard.

"Will, I hate to suggest this, but what would you think about the idea of me going down on the east side to try to get help?"

I'd be up there alone, with only the bears for company. But I, too, was tired of waiting.

"You mean take my truck and go to a phone somewhere?"

"Yeah. I'll get you a ride on a helicopter. That would be fun, eh?"

A wall of fog moved across the door,

sucking Matt's words out with it. The cold air swept in.

"Sure. Anything. Yeah, go ahead, Matt. Hey, close that door, will you? Yeah, it's a good idea. We've got to do something. We can't just rot away here waiting forever. I don't know what's happened at Faron's end."

I stared at the ceiling, trying grimly not to think about it.

"Will," Matt said. "I'm sure they're okay. The fog must be still too thick down there for the others to follow the trail up. It would've been easier for her on the way down."

I wasn't convinced. But it didn't much matter what either of us thought.

"Yeah, you're right. Go ahead then. I'll manage."

Matt stood silently debating for a moment, still framed by the door, now closed.

"Really," I told him. "I think you should go."

"I was just wondering," he said, "whether to take my pack or not. It's got my climbing gear, and extra clothes in it."

"Don't worry about it. Go ahead and take it, just in case. I know you're not going to desert me up here. You don't need to leave a deposit."

Matt snorted a laugh of appreciation. "Yup. Right. I'll take it, then."

He packed up quickly. A brief hug around my shoulders, and he straightened up to leave. Then he thought of something. He carried the half-full bucket of water from the counter, found a cup to go with it, and set them on the floor next to my bunk. Then he took the roasting pan I'd been using as a chamber pot out the door, brought it back in empty, and set it down on the floor beside the bucket.

"There," he said. "And there's plenty of firewood. The stove's full, so you may not even have to drag yourself out of bed. Do you think you can manage okay? I'll be back in a jiffy. Anchovies and double cheese?"

"Uh, hold the anchovies, thanks. Yeah, I'll manage."

"Bye, Will."

"Take care."

***

My pain had become rather dull, but we kept each other company just the same. I counted the hours till salvation. Matt left at close to one o'clock. By three he should have been striding with his long, strong legs down the road. I ticked away the minutes approaching four o'clock, the time I safely estimated as the hour of Matt's arrival at the truck.

My heart beat faster as I looked at my watch, riding with the imperceptible sweep of the long hand to the top of the hour. Two o'clock. Matt would be opening the door of the truck, throwing his pack into the passenger's seat, climbing in, reaching for the key—

—the key that was still in my pocket.

***

No doors left unopened. I tried them all again, and all were locked. I counted, in the dim light, three on each side. But no: there had been seven. I checked again: up one side of the hall (two locked knobs and a frozen latch), down the other (three locked knobs). Odd, but who was I to try to figure it out? The thing now was to get myself out. Or was this my final trial, the acceptance of fate closed forever from further possibility—my final home in an oblong box, with no exit?

Tired, I lay down, looking up at the ceiling, the too-close ceiling, imagining all the billions upon billions of stars out there somewhere,

somewhere. I had seen them once, through the open door of this one life. Would I be granted no more? I closed my eyes.

Chapter Eleven

Morning light grew slowly from the drizzling fog outside, through cabin windows misty white as a cocoon. Faron and I were still wrapped tightly in each other's arms, under our cozy quilt. Suze still slept snug in her bed, and Matt stirred slightly in his upper bunk.

We lingered long in bed, watching our breath hover in the air, enjoying the peace of the special time and place. I was as yet unconscious of the dreams I'd had; I was only aware of Faron warmly breathing beside me, and I savored that last exquisite touch of our bodies together. Suze moved in soon enough to make it a threesome—"a crowd," but idyllic in its own way. Then Matt bent his tousled head down from his bunk to greet us with a hoarse but cheery, "Good morning."

"Morning," said Faron.

"Hi—hi—hi," was Suze's high-pitched, staccato salutation.

"Did you sleep well?" I asked.

"Not too bad," Matt responded, "after that crashing of wood outside. I thought it might be a bear. Did you hear it?"

"Yes," I said, "and I thought of going out to see what it was, but decided I'd be better off behind that cabin door." Only as I said this did I remember my dreams.

I chose not to speak of them, as I had already set my sights on the return journey and wanted to proceed with our plans in a mood of confidence. I told myself that if we all survived such a night, we could certainly survive the day ahead.

Nothing to do then but plunge out of the covers and into cold clothes, eat a final breakfast together, pack up, and exit this box of dreams, into the icy gloom shrouding the ridges of Mirror Pass.

Holding Faron and Suze close for our last good-byes, I wondered—not for the last time— if we were being foolish and blind to ignore the weather.

"Maybe I should at least go down farther with you, till you find the actual trail."

Faron stuck to her familiar role. "No, that's okay. It might take us a long time to find it, or we might find it a long ways down. Matt would start to worry, and you might get lost on the way back up, like I did yesterday."

I nodded, agreeing with these points of logic.

She continued with her reassurances. "If you guys made it up on your side without any trail at all, then I should be all right finding my way down."

I wasn't sure if she was just trying to make it easy for me to stick to the plan. But I let her arguments stand, trusting her self-determination and my own power of choice, in the dim light of day.

One more kiss, and they vanished into the mists. I trudged back to the cabin to begin the descent on the other side of the mountain.

***

Matt and I were shortly hotfooting it down the east slope, leaving most of the foul weather behind. I felt, with some smug yet curious comfort, the truck keys in my pocket as we headed down. And with each step onto rock, mud, ice, or heather, I was careful to aim for stable footing, aware that one false step and a twisted ankle could leave me stranded. My leaps and bounds all managed to fall into place, and it took only an hour for us to reach the bottom.

Once on the road, we had another hour's walk to the truck. I began to recall in more detail the succession of nightmares, which led to regretful second thoughts about my headstrong decision to let Faron and Suze go unguided down the western slope. I told Matt about the soul-wrenching dreams...omitting that farce of sexual jealousy.

Matt said, "Well, I guess it's out of our hands now, buddy."

"Is that meant to console me?"

He didn't answer.

"Do you think we should have let Faron and Suze go into the whiteout like that?"

Now it was *we*. I wondered how my hiking partner would react to the implication of joint responsibility. He took it without flinching.

"I had my doubts, but I did go along with it.

Now that I hear those nightmares of yours, though, I must admit—I'm not so sure anymore."

"How much do dreams matter, anyway? Do you believe in prophecies? Those different unhappy endings can't all happen."

"That's a point. Maybe they were just warnings of what could happen."

"Yeah, no matter what we decided…letting them go down the other side; staying up there in the pass…."

"I see what you mean," Matt said. "At some point, you just have to do the best you can."

We paused to greet a Stellar's jay who perched beside us atop a precipitous drop to the gorge below. Matt said it was a good omen.

The truck, we knew, was parked just around the next bend in the road, across the last washout. But the runoff had swollen to a considerably greater depth and force after the overnight rain. So we chose to cross this time with the aid of a rope sling, which we set up to ferry our packs across.

With dry clothes waiting in the truck, we decided to keep our boots and pants on as we waded into the waist-deep, icy current. Luckily our poplar banister was still there for us to hang onto as we fought the turbulence on the way across.

We came to the truck with final sighs of relief, briskly changed, and jumped into the cab. But around the next bend in the road, we were forced to wonder where we'd taken a wrong turn. There was another major washout where the previous day, harmless inches of water had trickled over the road. It was nearly as wide and deep as the one we'd just waded through. Could we have somehow bypassed the real road? No, the truth remained: this was a brand-new washout—except that it had a certain grim familiarity for me, created overnight by the combined deluge of the storm and the melting snows. Logs that had formed a foundation for the roadbed were strewn about in the water, among the large rocks downstream, like so many pick-up sticks.

We got out of the truck, gaping in disbelief. The creek that roared in front of us was a good ten feet across and two feet deep, and full of boulders in such irregular array that, except for the old logs, and the road that plunged abruptly into the torrent on either side, one would never know that a road had ever crossed there.

Little chance of making it across now. We paced back and forth along the rocky bank. Our minds raced from one unreasonable solution to another.

We could go for the crossing, hoping for freakish luck to bounce us from boulder to boulder and over to the other side. If we didn't make it, the truck would have to be left in the creek until we got a tow truck up here.

But it would be a thirty-kilometer walk to Columbiana, I pointed out, and it was already mid-afternoon. If we phoned from there for a tow truck, it might not make it past the other swollen washouts farther along the road; it would, however, coming all the way from Inverness, cost plenty—maybe close to the value of my stranded truck.

"Hey," Matt said, backing off a little, "it's your truck. Whatever you want to do."

***

Maybe, I considered, I could just ditch the ill-fated Ford, at least temporarily. Then I'd have to somehow make it through the rest of the planting season without a truck—and all my gear for camping and planting, the variety of clothes for weather ranging from snow to burning heat, the spare boots, shovels, sleeping bags, and tent. I could plan to return later in the summer with the Dodge to pull it out…what was left of it by then.

We desperately plumbed our reserves of luck and surveyed the possible angles of an alternative crossing. Twenty feet upstream the creek was wider and somewhat shallower, though still it swelled with a wild force that made the prospects of success seem madly slim. The only hope might be to build up the deepest holes in the creek bed there with fresh layers of rock. The current was strong enough to make loose boulders roll, however, so a log dam, supported by a row of well-placed rocks, would have to be installed first. It just might work.

We would also have to mine the approaches on both sides to remove the large rocks and log-ends that otherwise prevented access to the existing road. That operation would provide plenty of fill material beside the stream.

It was still a gamble, and it would take hours. If we invested our afternoon in such work and then stranded the truck in midstream, we'd be left without enough daylight, energy, or food for the walk to Columbiana. Either way, botching it like that, or ditching the truck now and continuing on foot, we'd be faced with a six-hour walk...unless the gamble worked.

"So, what do you think?" I asked Matt.

"It's your truck."

"Oh, hell," I said, with a shrug of my shoulders. "Let's go for it."

We spent the next three hours hardly talking, just working doggedly to throw and drop and nudge rock after rock into place, building up the streambed, wading and digging, smoothing and widening the approaches.

At last the job was done well enough—we hoped. The water still rushed over the rocks about a foot deep, but without its former turbulence, as the boulders now fit together in a relatively even pattern under the current. The large tires and high-riding frame of the truck would be put to the test, but with a good head of steam, we just might make it.

I hopped in behind the wheel, with my adrenalin starting to flow. Matt posted himself on the upstream side to watch where the wheels were headed. It was going to be hard for me to see where I was going, and I'd only have one chance.

The engine revved smoothly; I gunned it, clutching the steering wheel, and bounced the truck through the current, churning over our makeshift roadbed to dry land on the other side. Matt trotted down to the truck and pointed back to the creek with eyes wide.

"Man, you just made it," he said. "Your right rear wheel took out that log dam just as it passed over. Good thing you had some momentum, or you'd still be back in the creek."

***

Matt and I arrived at Columbiana just in time for our four-thirty phone call to the company office. I also tried my home number to see if Faron had arrived yet. There was no answer, and once more I began to worry.

"It's still a little early yet," Matt reassured me. "It must have been slow going with that load she was carrying."

"Yeah, I guess you're right."

Back on the road, I had to wonder...would we really be able to enjoy a celebratory supper tonight? In fact, would we even get as far as Inverness? My eyes followed the needle of the fuel gauge down to E, and below.

"Maybe I should have tried Ron's while we were at the phone, to see if she stopped there on her way home. Or maybe her sister's place."

"Hey, we'll be in town in a few minutes. It's all downhill from here."

As soon as we gassed up and parked, I headed for the pay phone. Matt went on to a restaurant across the street called The Meeting Place.

Faron answered, her voice vibrantly alive. She and Suze were all right, but on the way down, she'd been lost.

"Oh, Faron," I told her, sick at heart. "I should have gone with you farther to find that trail."

"I don't know how much that would have helped, really. I just couldn't see a thing. And I was completely soaked, and shivering, and my pants were torn, and Suze was crying...." Faron herself started to cry on the phone while she told me the rest.

For hours she'd wandered through the untracked brush, until, at the limit of her endurance, she decided to bushwhack straight downhill, leaving the backpack behind so as to save what little strength she had left for carrying Suze.

My grief at being partly responsible for her nightmarish ordeal was balanced by a final elation that they'd survived. The backpack could stay there forever, even with our down quilts inside, as a monument to what might have been.

"But I know where I left it," Faron said. "Under a certain tree—"

"Oh, great. Under a tree."

"I don't think it would be that hard to find. I made a little stone cairn, to mark the trail where I came onto it, straight downhill from the pack. I bet we could find it—"

We. Now that sounded more promising. Maybe it would be fun to go back there together. We could take along some flagging tape and mark the hillside as we traversed it, looking for the pack. Suze would enjoy a little picnic out there...if the bugs weren't too bad in July.

We told each other good-bye, and I left the phone booth with a spring in my step, to cross the street to The Meeting Place.

Chapter Twelve

Morning dawned through the nearby window, and my eyelids pulled slowly open. Faron still slept beside me curled under the covers; I'd tossed them off during the night and now felt cold in the chill morning air. I could see that Suze still slept peacefully in her bed. I pulled the bedclothes back over me and snuggled closer to Faron.

It was clear out, likely to be another scorching July day once the sun came out in force. This was to be the day we would go back to Mirror Pass together, to see if the bears and squirrels had left us anything of the backpack. If we could find it at all. If the Tumbler Creek road was still negotiable. If I didn't get called back to work while we sat down to breakfast. If the good weather held.

About the Author

Nowick Gray writes in a variety of genres, each work teasing the dynamics of choice among multiple realities: whether romantic relationships, plot endings, murder suspects, virtual worlds, alternate timelines, narrative loops, stylistic colorings...

Nowick works as a freelance copy editor, plays flute and performs West African and Brazilian drumming, and enjoys nature photography and swimming. His various passions and interests span several personal websites and blogs, with the hub at Cougar WebWorks - http://cougarwebworks.com

Educated at Dartmouth College and the University of Victoria, he taught in Inuit villages in the Arctic before carving out a homestead in the BC mountains. In more recent years he calls Victoria home, while wintering in tropical locations.

Made in the USA
Charleston, SC
05 September 2013